The Elves and the Shoemaker

retold for easy reading
by VERA SOUTHGATE M A B Com

ill  N

Once upon a time there lived a shoemaker and his wife.

The man was a good shoemaker and he worked hard, yet he and his wife were very poor.

As time went on, they grew poorer and poorer.

At last the day came when all
the shoemaker had left was
enough leather to make one
pair of shoes.

That evening, before he went
to bed, the shoemaker cut out
a pair of shoes from the leather.
Then he left them on his workbench
ready to sew next morning.

The next day the shoemaker got up
early and went into his workshop
to make the shoes.

But when he got there, he couldn't
believe his eyes! On his bench,
instead of the leather that he had
left cut out, he found a beautiful
pair of shoes, already made.

The shoemaker picked up the shoes and looked carefully at them. They were neatly made, with not one bad stitch in them.

He showed the shoes to his wife. "I have never seen such a well made pair of shoes," she said. "They are perfect."

But the shoemaker and his wife were puzzled. They could not think who had sewn the shoes.

The same morning, a lady came into the shop to buy a pair of shoes.

The shoemaker showed her the pair he had found on his bench. "These are the most beautifully made shoes I have ever seen," she said.

The lady tried on the shoes and they fitted perfectly. She was pleased with the shoes and paid the shoemaker well for them.

With the money, the shoemaker was able to buy leather for two pairs of shoes.

That night, before he went to bed, he cut out the shoes. He left them on his workbench ready to sew in the morning.

The next day, the shoemaker got
up early and went into his shop
to make the shoes. But once again
he had a surprise. Now there were
two pairs of fine shoes on his
workbench.

He took the shoes in his hands and
looked carefully at them. Once
more the shoes were perfectly made.
Not a stitch was out of place.

That morning, a man came into
the shop to buy some shoes.

The shoemaker showed him the two
pairs of shoes that he had found
on his bench. The man said,
"I have never seen such well made
shoes."

He was so pleased
with them
that he
bought both
pairs of shoes. He
paid the shoemaker
twice the usual price.

And so it went on. Every night,
the shoemaker cut out some shoes
and left them on his workbench.

Every morning, he found the shoes,
all neatly made.

Many rich customers came to
his shop to buy these perfect shoes.
Before long the shoemaker and
his wife were rich.

One evening, not long before
Christmas, the shoemaker and
his wife sat eating dinner.

"We still do not know who sews
the shoes for us," the shoemaker
said. "Shall we stay up tonight
to see who has been helping us?"

His wife thought that this was a
very good idea, so she lit a candle
and they went into the workshop.

The shoemaker and his wife hid in
a corner of the room and waited
quietly.

For a long time nothing happened.

Then, just as the clock struck twelve, the door of the workshop opened and in ran two little elves, dressed in rags.

The elves jumped onto the workbench and took up the shoes that were cut out. They began to stitch and sew and hammer. They worked so neatly and so quickly that the shoemaker could hardly believe his eyes.

The elves worked without stopping until all the shoes were finished. Then they ran quickly away.

At breakfast the next morning the shoemaker asked his wife, "How can we thank these little elves, who have made us so rich and so happy?"

"I know what we can do," said his wife. "We can make them new clothes and shoes. Their own clothes are ragged and their feet are bare."

During the evenings that followed, the shoemaker and his wife began to make new clothes for the elves.

The shoemaker chose the softest leather he could find. He cut out two of the tiniest pairs of shoes you have ever seen. Then he stitched the shoes as carefully as he could.

The shoemaker's wife cut out two white shirts, two small green jackets and two pairs of trousers to match. She sewed them with tiny stitches.

She made two little caps, each with a feather in it.

She also knitted two pairs of little white stockings.

By Christmas Eve the tiny clothes and shoes were finished.

The shoemaker cleared the leather and tools from his workbench. He and his wife laid their presents on the bench, instead of the usual work.

Then they hid themselves as they had done before and waited to see what the elves would do.

Just as the clock struck twelve,

the door opened quietly, as before.

The two elves came running in.

They still wore old clothes and

their feet were blue with cold.

They jumped onto the bench, ready

to start work at once. But there

was no leather on the bench, only

the tiny presents.

The elves were astonished at first
and then they were delighted. In no
time at all they were out of their
old clothes.

Then, talking and laughing, they
dressed themselves in the beautiful
new clothes – the green jacket and
trousers, the white shirt and
stockings, the soft leather shoes
and the little caps with the feathers
that nodded as they laughed.

In their delight, the little elves
skipped and jumped over chairs
and benches.

Then they joined hands and danced
around, as they sang:

"Now we are boys so fine to see,

We need no longer cobblers be."

At last they danced happily out of
the door.

The shoemaker and his wife never saw the little elves again. But, from that time, good luck was always with them.

They were rich and happy for the rest of their lives.